AND THEN SOME

A Ruben Kane Novel

By

Eddie J Martin

Copyright © **2016 by Eddie J Martin**

All rights reserved.

Published in **the USA**

ISBN-13:978-0996533959

10: 0996533958

No part of this book may be reproduced in any form unless written permission is granted from the author or publisher. No electronic reproductions, information storage, or retrieval systems may be used or applied to any part of this book without written permission.

Due to the variable conditions, materials, and individual skills, the publisher, author, editor, translator, transcriber, and/or designer disclaim any liability for loss or injury resulting from the use or interpretation of any information presented in this publication. No liability is assumed for damages resulting from the use of the information contained herein.

And then some

For Barbara Smith (Porgy),

My cousin, friend and confidant. Your friendship will always be cherished.

PROLOGUE

And then some

MY NAME IS Ruben Kane. In 1938, Cleveland Ohio, I was a private detective. At age 42 and black I was doing all right. I had a new car, money in the bank, and an office on the 13th floor of one of the most exclusive buildings in town. My reputation was known as Far East in the hood to the west in the white neighborhood. From the poor to the rich, from the hookers to the pimps... A non-discriminatory dick—that's me. No job I won't take; no problem I won't attempt. Are there jobs that I should have passed on? You batcha.

Have you ever wondered what would happen if the tides were somehow turned? I mean, what if little kids ruled the world? It would be a happier world, I would imagine. And what if pigs could really fly? We'd have bacon on the fly. Then again, what if the pimp's roles were reversed to that

6

of the hookers and the hookers to that of the pimps, what would it be like?

The hookers beating up on the pimp's every time they look at them in the wrong way, taking their money, and screwing them whenever… And in turn, they end up working for them. A hell of a predicament, wouldn't you say? But I'm only saying, what if?

CHAPTER 1

COLEMAN HOWKINS was playing "Some Other Spring" on the box, my feet were on my desk, and my fingers were folded behind my head. My coffee cup was half full of Jim Bean whiskey, due to the ice melting. Occasionally, I looked out the window, 13 floors below, watching the trolley cars go by and the people of Cleveland do their daily thing, like going to work, home, or dinner, and watching them walk through the park, which was on the other side of the Boulevard. I must admit, I had a great view and the price was right.

My office came by way of me doing a job for this banker, and he wanted to show his appreciation. He had this rental property, so he let me have it for one dollar—for life. He was appreciative. I've been here for a few years now, and I even got a secretary. Rita! She's been with me for about as long as I've had the office. Rita is an illegal immigrant of Mexican descent, who's been in the country for several years with no job, so I hired her on the QT. Plus, she works cheap. You've heard of private eyes having secretaries who are 5 foot 5, blond-haired person, blue-eyed, 40-26-38, with asses that won't quit—you know what I'm talking about.

And then some

Rita is nothing like that; she's 5 foot 2, 250 pounds, with huge breasts where she keeps her stilettos. She has long black hair, is very cute and talks plenty of shit. Rita and I got along right from the start. She walked into my office and said, "RK," (she calls me RK when no one is around) "I'm going home now, is there anything you need before I leave?"

"Yeah, Rita. Maybe you could refresh my drink before you go. No coffee, two cubes of ice, and the rest JB." After doing that, Rita said, "Look here what I found, an almost full pack of Camel cigarettes. I thought you gave up on these things long ago?"

"I have, Rita; can't you tell that's an old pack?"

She looked at them again and said. "I guess you were on stakeout when you had these, nothing else to do, right? There's a penis on this camel, did you know that? I know they didn't come that way."

"Just throw them in the trash, Rita, and good night."

"See you tomorrow, RK."

That Rita, always coming up with some bullshit. Besides, that was one of my better projects. When you're out on stakeout like that you have to find something to occupy your time, so why not put a dick on a camel? He looked kind of sad standing there without it. After Rita left, I resumed my thoughts where I left off. The last few days have been relatively quiet, but the last case was enough drama for the next two years. Murder, sex, and romance—it had it all. This case contained everything. If someone wanted to, they could write a book about what happened. And, I have to think how something like that could have happened; I can hardly believe it myself. It started out like this: I spent the night with a girl I had met the night before at the Cave Club. We had meant to get together long before but never had. On this night, we made it our business to do just that and I said, "Look, I could sit here half the night, filling you full of alcohol, talking shit,

12

and trying to get you into bed when we know that's where things are leading anyway. So, I'll tell you what, how about this? We forgo all that and head straight for the house."

"But it's still early, you want to leave now?"

"The longer to love you, my dear."

"I don't do breakfasts; they have never been my strong point."

"Don't worry about it, what you do will make up for all that..."

"You say that to say what?"

"To say, let's do it again, Sam."

"You can be so crazy. Why haven't we hooked up long before now?"

"Well, it's like this, Beverly. It's always been when you were coming in and I was going out, and vice versa. But I've always wanted those drawls. Have you ever seen yourself from behind? Oh, my God!"

When I left Beverly's house, I headed for Skippy's diner. I don't know about her, but I had to eat. After ham and eggs, home fries with onions, toast, and coffee, I was ready for the day. When I came out of Skippy's, it was a tossup whether to go to my apartment, which I shared with my wife, or to the office. I decided on the office. I would call my wife, Ella, later to see if I received any messages. My wife and I have on arrangement; she goes her way and I go mine. It's been that way for a couple of years now. There is very little conversation between us and absolutely no sex. How do you make love to a woman you can't touch? One day, I expect one of us will say good-bye and hit the road but right now, it benefits both of us to stay right where we are.

CHAPTER 2

IN MY 1940 Buick, I noticed the gas tank was on empty so I stopped by the service station. I told Fred, the attendant, to give me two dollars' worth of Hi-test and check the tires, oil, and water, and wash the windows while I went to the washroom. When I returned, Fred told me the bill. I checked the gas gauge and noticed it wasn't where I thought it should be and said to Fred, "$2.75? I barely got three quarters of a tank. How much you are selling this stuff for, anyway?"

"Gas just went up, RK. It's now $.21 a gallon."

You bull-shiting me! Gas at these prices, should be a law. No one can afford gas at these prices. I'm thinking about you pulling this shit out of my gas tank right now."

"Hell, RK. Don't get so upset. In a few years, they tell me it's going to be twice that."

"Here, take your money and let me get the fuck away from here. $.21 a gallon, ridiculous."

Rita was at her desk doing her nails when I walked in. I must admit, for a big woman, she was looking damn good—that or I'm just a horny old man at 42.

"I didn't think you were coming in today, RK."

"I just can't stay away, Rita. Give me a few days' rest and I'm back. Any coffee?"

"Rest! You been resting for the last few days."

"Damn, Rita, you're right."

"Right enough for a raise?"

"We're not talking raise right now, Rita. Maybe later."

"Raymond called. He said he needed to talk to you and may have a case."

After Rita poured a half cup of coffee for me, I filled the rest with Jim Bean. Can't have coffee without a little hook in it. Raymond is the local barber from my old neighborhood. He's been around forever. He used to cut us kids' hair, including most of the people in the hood. I moved out but I still go back from time to time, not only for the cut, but Raymond is our all-seeing eye; he knows everything that goes on. They say if you want to know something, check with your bartender, shoeshine boy, or barber. At 64 years old and 300 pounds, Raymond used to be one hell of a man but is now mostly just fat. He's still something, wearing that smock and visor with half cut bifocals over his nose. He looks just like a barber should look.

"Raymond, how's it hanging?"

"Say, RK. I'm okay, wanted to talk to you. Something came up that I believe would be right up your alley."

"I'm listening, Raymond. Shoot!"

"I received a call from one of our local pimps. Get this: three of his girls jumped him, beat the hell out of him, and advised him to get the hell out of Cleveland. Don't laugh, RK. That's the same reaction I had until I saw his face. If they did that to him, I'd take their advice. He wasn't the only one, two others were also beat down by their ladies. No one seems to know what's gotten into them. A couple of the guys tried to go back on the block and gain control but as soon as they showed up and jumped on one of the girls, five to ten others showed up to her defense. The last guy that showed up was beaten up and they took his automobile."

"So, what do you think is going on, Raymond?"

"They think it's a conspiracy. The girls have all gotten together and are going their separate ways without them. The pimps—five of them—want you to be an intermediary with the women."

"How many women are we talking about?"

"No less than 50. This is serious, RK. They think it is, anyway. They're willing to pay you a nice piece of change for doing this for them."

"And I guess they're paying you a little bit if I take the case?"

"We're not talking about that, RK. Let's just say that I'm happy with the arrangement."

"When can I meet these fellows, Raymond?"

"Then you'll take the case, RK?"

"I'll talk to them and if it feels right, then I'll take the case."

"Okay, RK, great. I'll tell them and will set up a meeting and call you back."

And that's how it started. I should have known, 50 women and hookers at that. Pimps can't control them. Something bad was about to happen; I could feel it.

Raymond called me back two days later and told me the location of the meeting for the guys: east side of Cleveland in a warehouse that had been remodeled into apartments. It so happened that it was the same apartment Smooth used to occupy. Smooth was one of them; he flew the coop just before the war to keep from going. The last I heard from him, he was in Alaska. The apartment was an old warehouse that Smooth had remodeled. There was one elevator big enough for a car, you just drove in from the street and it took you right up to the third floor.

CHAPTER 3

And then some

IF YOU WALKED into on empty warehouse, here is what you'd see: a skylight 50 feet above, windows 15 to 20 feet every 100 feet apart, five cars parked every which way, 10 bedrooms and seven baths, two couches, three plush chairs, a pool table, and a 25-foot bar that had a whole in the lower part that was never repaired. There were rumors that one of Smooth's girlfriends shot a hitman from New Iberia, Louisiana through that bar. They say it was a double barrel and she let him have both boroughs for trying to kill Smooth. Five men were there when Ruben drove in and parked. One of them came over and introduced himself, saying, "My name is Danyon. I'll introduce you to the others, if that's all right?" Danyon was approximately 5'8 and 160 pounds, with a dark brown complexion and a micelle haircut. He was wearing a gabardine light brown suit with a silk shirt open at the collar, a white handkerchief in the breast pocket of the suit, and dark brown loafers with no socks. He also had a golden chain around his neck with a cross attached. Rabbit sat over on the couch. He runs the three hotels in downtown Cleveland and has 13 girls working for him 24/7. Pickle, next to him, has 10 girls working the river resort area and 5 girls working for him. Pickle was wearing a black suit, with a matching shirt and bowtie and was also the one that was bandaged up around his head and right hand. Rainbow has the downtown bus station and train station. He was wearing a tan suit with a matching shirt, stud son shoes, and a fedora. He has eight girls working for him. Rainbow looks white but believe me, he's black. Trinidad has the airport scene and 20 girls working for him. He has the larger area; thereby, has the most girls. He's from Jamaica. He was wearing a white suit, white sandals, and no socks or shirt. All five were exclusively dressed—like pimps, you might say. "What do you know,

And then some

Mr. Kane?"

"Call me RK. Not very much, only what Raymond told me. You fellows have been having problems with your employees, can you tell me what brought that on?"

"We don't rightly know, RK. First, Pickle said that one of my girls started giving me some back talk, then another one. We can't have that, so I bashed her upside the head, no big thing. This time, she bangs me right back upside my head, so I started getting down on her ass and the next thing I know, the other girls started swinging on me with everything but the kitchen sink. I started running out my own pad. I only went back when I knew they were on the job."

"About the same thing happened to me," the guy named Rabbit said. "I jumped one's ass because she didn't bring in the money I expected, so I started to go upside her head, which was a mistake. I did it in front of five of my other girls and they jumped me. They told me there would be no more of that shit and that as soon as they work it out, there will be another arrangement, whereby I'll be working for them. You hear that shit? I'll be working for them. You ever heard of such a thing? The pimp working for the hookers."

"I take it the same thing happened to each of you?"

"That's only the half of it. They fucked up a couple of our cars, ripped up our clothes—some of us just have what's on our backs— and bank books. I think that was the first thing to go. And as you can guess, they control the purse strings."

"Okay, okay I get it. Where do I come in?"

"We want you to try and talk to them and get things back to where they were. We are willing to forgive and forget."

"That's all, no retaliation of any kind. You're willing to settle for that? You know if you do that, your reputation won't be worth a dime. There is nowhere in the city you would be able to go. Nowhere in the state."

"We know that, RK, but we got a plan. If this works out, with you talking to the girls, then after a reasonable amount of time, we figure things will go back to normal and then we'll lower the boom on them and they'll be under our thumb for ever after," Danyon said.

"And what if I don't succeed?"

"Well," Rainbow said, "we'll just have to go to plan B."

"And what would plan B consist of? Do I wanna know?"

"We'll just have to start knocking a few of them off."

"Look, I'll have no part in murder but I will talk to the girls for you. Now, let's talk frankly."

Two days later, I received a call from Danyon. He contacted one of the girls and they agreed to meet with me. The plan is to meet one of them at the train station and she would take me to the meeting place with the others. I had 24 hours before 9 PM the next night. I am to come alone.

The next day came. I had spent the night at my girlfriend's apartment. Most nights, when I'm not on a case, that's where I am. Freda has asked me several times to move in with her but after living with Ella for years and it not being so swell, I'm not about to move in with another woman. Plus, I believe it'll mess up a beautiful relationship. After leaving Freda's place, I thought I'd drop by Mama Sue's, get dinner, and then head over to the

29

apartment I shared with my wife, change my clothes, say hello to her, and then go to the meeting. The first thing that I noticed when I walked into the apartment was that the kitchen light was on and it felt cold in there—not physically cold, but the feeling you get when you have a loss in your life. I called out to Ella and got no answer. I looked around the place, walked into my room and started to take my clothes off and take a shower. Once I was done, I got dressed, walked into the kitchen, and took my Jim Bean and a glass out of the cabinet. I poured a half glass standing up and drank it. I put the bottle back and the glass in the sink and was about to cut the light off and leave when I noticed it—a note on the kitchen table, folded in half with my name on it. I picked it up and read.

Ruben,

Eddie J Martin

Just wanted to let you know that I'll be moving on. There seems to be no future for us and I'm miserable and I'm sure you are too.

I wish you all the best, take care.

  Ella

I took the bottle back out the cabinet, retrieved my glass out of the sink, poured another drink and didn't stop until it reached the brim. I drank it down in one swoop, sat down at the table, and read the note again. Ain't that a bitch? It finally happened. I'm gonna be lonely in the old place now that she's gone. Never thought it would happen. Well, I'll be damned. I poured myself another drink, only half a glass this time. Hell, I got a job to go to.

CHAPTER 4

THE LADY I met at the train station didn't look like any hooker I had ever seen before, and I've been around. Her hair was up in a bun, and she was wearing pearl earrings and a necklace. She had large blue eyes, a long nose and very white teeth. Her lips were the color of cherries and showcased her red hair. He was wearing a gray tweed business suit and high black heels. If I didn't know any better, I would have guessed she was either a business woman, model, or steward. Overall, one fine mother jumper. "Mr. Kane, my name is Ingram. I was asked to pick you up and escort you to the meeting place. Were you aware that you were being followed?"

"I was not, Ms. Ingram. Is there something we can do about that?"

"We anticipated this, with the kinds of people we are dealing with. Come with me please. Hurry please!" We half-walked and half-ran to the train platform to catch a train that was just leaving the station. We boarded the last coach just in time to see two men rushing out of the station.

"You know them?" Ingram said.

"No, never saw them before."

We got off ten miles outside of Cleveland. Outside the station, a 1940 four door black Packard picked us up with two more ladies inside, but they were dressed entirely different. They were wearing black pants suits down to their shoes and from what I saw later, if they were hookers, they were dressed the wrong way for business. A few miles out, the car stopped and Ingram said, "I'm sorry, Mr. Kane, but I'll have to put this hood over your head." We drove what seemed like 30 to 45 minutes, most of it was paved road but a lot was gravel. We passed over at least two bridges and under one tunnel bridge. We eventually pulled off into some type of yard and into a building, which I later found out was a barn. Ingram helped me out of the car and took off my hood, and after my eyes adjusted to the light, I thought I'd died and gone to heaven. Girls, women everywhere. They were up in the rafters, standing on ladders, sitting on hoods of cars, laying around on the floor, and in haystacks. There were white ones, black ones, Chinese and others of all nationalities. There had to be at least fifty or sixty of them.

All I could do was smile.

An older lady approached me and said, "Stop drooling, Mr. Kane, you're here for business, not pleasure."

I wanted to ask about benefits but thought better of it.

"My name is Sue Lynn and I am the spokesperson for the group. To answer your questions before you ask, we are over 50 strong, and growing. We cover the Cleveland area, including the airport. I will not go through our names but I'm sure you've seen some of us around. The only reason you are here is that some of the ladies feel they don't want to go it alone—that is, without their pimps. The others feel they don't want to be hit every time they turn around. Every time they don't bring in a certain amount of money, or even when they do, they see very little of it. So,

And then some

Mr. Kane, you're here to convince us why we should stay. Are you ready, Mr. Kane? You have the floor!"

"Ladies, first, I want you to know that I'm not here to convince you of anything, I'm here to deliver a message from your formal employers and that is simply this: if you come back, then all is forgiven. They're willing to forget and forgive. Just bring back the bank books you took, replace the clothes you ripped up, and work longer hours to replace the damage you did to their cars."

The uproar from the women could be heard for half a mile. A few of the women started coming toward me. Miss Lynn held up her hands and the noise died down.

"Now, ladies, don't blame Mr. Kane for the message. After all, he is only the messenger. And this is what we wanted, a dialogue with our ex-employers. Now, we know the reason we are here. Are there any doubts why we're doing what we're doing? Would anyone like to vote to stay with these people after listening to Mr. Kane?" The entire group raised their voices in an overwhelming 'no'.

"Mr. Kane, you heard the group, but before you go, we want to send you back with a counter offer. We want you to tell them to come work for us. We'll let them keep their present position, but with stipulations. No disrespecting us, no slapping us around, no taking all our money and only giving us what they think we should have. No screwing us anytime they like. On the other hand, we will pay them a decent salary. Mr. Kane, we don't expect you to remember all of this, that's why we had it written down for you. Take it back to them and tell them what you saw."

12:45 AM I was dropped off at the Cave Club. I took a seat at the bar and ordered two double shots of JB. I downed them one after the other and ordered two more.

"Damn RK," the bartender said. "What's up with you tonight? I've never seen you put them away like that before."

All I can tell you, Jed, is I need this and before it's all over, I think I may need six more just like it."

I woke up the next morning in my apartment. I don't know how I managed to get there. My head was throbbing and my body was hurting. I half-crawled out of bed and made it to the bathroom and threw up. I started walking toward the kitchen and hollowed out, "Ella, Ella! The coffee ready yet?"

When I got to the kitchen, the chairs were all disarranged and knocked over, the cabinet doors were open, and my bottle of JB was on the floor and leaking alcohol. Then, I saw the note and I remembered that Ella was gone.

After a shower and a change of clothes, I stopped off at Skippy's diner for some breakfast and a heap of coffee. From there, I headed for the office. Rita wasn't there but she left me a note stating she was taking the day off. I made my own coffee and prepared to make the call I dreaded to make.

Before I left the barn and Ms. Lynn, I asked her about the ladies walking around all in black—they didn't look like or act like the others. She told me they were the SWAK team (Seal With a Kiss), and that they handle all their trash. "They are all ex-military personnel and hookers; they are good at what they do. Make no mistake, Mr. Kane, we are deadly serious to get that across to your clients."

And then some

The next day, I called Danyon and told him I should meet with all five of them as soon as possible. We decided on that night at 9 PM. I wanted to give them time to arrive, so I got there at 9:10. When I arrived, they were all there.

"Lay it on us," Pickle said. "What did the bitches have to say?"

"They rejected your offer. In fact, they sent you a counter offer. They asked that you come work for them. They would pay you a decent salary, but many things would have to change. In addition, they would not return your bank books or repair your ripped clothing nor your cars. They said a lot more, so they wrote it down for you to read it for yourself."

After passing out the letters and them showing their outrage, they paid and thanked me, and I was dismissed. Despite not being impressed with the counter offer, they never said what they were going to do—nothing nice, I'd bet.

The next day, I put the cash in our office safe, which was under the desk in the floor. I paid Rita her two weeks' salary and caught up on all my bills. Bernie called about missing the number the night before by one and asked if I wanted to play tonight. Freda called and I asked her if she wanted to go to dinner. For a Wednesday, this week was starting out quiet. Monday with the hookers, Tuesday with the pimps, and Wednesday with Freda. Made some coin to last me the month, not bad. At 1 PM, I made it to Skippy's diner for lunch. Liver and onions, mashed potatoes and beans, a roll, and an iced tea. I didn't want to put it on too thick or Freda would think I'd already eaten. On the way out, the diner and as I was getting into my Buick, I ran into Charles the paper carrier. "RK, what's up? Hey, let me ask you something. Have you felt something different around the hood in the last week?"

"Like what Charles?"

"Like the ladies of the night, I can't put my finger on it but they seem different. And the boys—the pimps—I haven't seen them around."

"No, Charles. I haven't noticed anything like that. It's just your imagination."

The quiet before the storm, I thought. All hell's about to break loose. I heard about it first from Rita when I came into the office Friday morning. "RK, have you read the paper yet?"

"No, I missed it this morning. What did it say?"

"One of the street girls was found dead in the river."

"Oh shit," I said. Rita bought my coffee and I put it aside, grabbed my bottle of JB, and took a big hit. I poured a portion in my coffee cup. After reading the paper, Rita asked me if I knew her.

And then some

"No, I didn't. But I knew of her, and she has friends."

That Tuesday, I received a call from Ms. Lynn. She informed me that the funeral for the girl who was murdered would be Thursday, and that I should contact my clients and tell them they're invited.

"Ms. Lynn, they are no longer my clients. I only had that one-time employment with them."

"All right then, Mr. Kane, we're employing you to contact them and deliver this message. Don't forget: Thursday 10 AM."

I called Danyon and relayed the message to him and asked him if he and his friends had anything to do with the murder. He didn't answer.

"Well, it doesn't matter, you are being accused of it anyway. The ladies are not going to take this laying down. I think you guys just started a war."

"A war with a bunch of hookers. Who do you think will win that one?"

"These hookers are united and they seem to have their stuff together."

"Thanks for thinking about us, RK, and thanks for the message, but we can handle it from here."

"RK, this is Raymond, you heard about one of the girls getting hit?"

"Yeah, I have."

"Any idea who the hitters were?"

"Yeah I've got an idea but I'm not saying. If I know, others will also know."

"Either things are going back to normal after this or all hell's going to break loose."

"Whatever happens, I don't think it'll be until after the funeral."

"Are you involved in this, RK?"

"Not this time, Raymond. Not this time."

CHAPTER 5

ON THURSDAY MORNING AT 10 AM I was at the funeral, along with 100 ladies of the night. The ladies in black were also there; the persons—the pimps—were not. Most of the ladies acknowledged me and I them. Ms. Lynn approached me and asked if I had delivered their message. I said I had and she just shook her head. Before the funeral was over, word went around that another girl was found in the East River. Ms. Lynn let it be known that there would be a meeting with SWAK. On Friday morning, Spider called Danyon and reported that the hit on girl number two had been carried out and they had received their payment.

"Do you need anything else?" he asked.

"Not until we hear from them. They should know by now that we're serious."

"Have you a way to contact them?"

"Yeah, we'll use RK again."

"Do you need any more help?"

"Just Otis, he's all I need. At 6 foot four and 325 pounds, he loves to hurt folks, he'll do."

"Okay I'll be in touch."

On Friday night, the meeting of the five took place, but only four showed up; Pickle was missing.

"Ruben, this is Lieutenant Jeffries."

"First thing Monday morning, this is a surprise. What can I do for you lieutenant?"

"I thought maybe you could help me out. We found one of the boys in his car off Cedar and 79th St. with his throat cut. He goes by the name of Robert Marshall, a.k.a. Pickle. What can you tell me about him?"

"I've heard of him, lieutenant, but that's about all."

"What have you heard, Ruben? Anything will help."

"Just that he ran a few girls and was doing pretty good."

"Have you heard any scuttle between the hookers and their pimps?"

"Now, how would I know anything like that, lieutenant? You know I tend to mind my own business."

"We've been hearing there is something going down, and we've been picking up very few streetwalkers lately. That means there are no pimps to get them out. If there's anyone who might know what's going on, it would be you."

"If I knew anything, I would tell you. You know that, lieutenant."

"Well, keep me in mind if you hear anything."

On Wednesday night, Rainbow was at the Ebony Club trying to recruit new prospects. The girl he was whispering to was in her teens and seemed to be going for what he was putting down. Within the hour, they got up to leave and walked to Rainbow's vehicle, which was parked in the alley. He opened the passenger side door for her and was about to get in on his side, when three ladies in black blocked him in. One of the women covered his hand with hers as he grabbed the door handle. He looked at all three and said, "Can I help you?" The one that was to his left, slapped him upside the head with a blackjack, while the other two started cutting and stabbing him. He managed to open the door and get in the vehicle but when he was about to put the key in the ignition, the girl in the car started stabbing him. Not a single area on his upper body was not penetrated, cut or hit. The medics told the police that he could have died, but that he would only be out of commission for the next six weeks.

On Thursday, I received a call from Danyon. "RK, did you contact those bitches?"

"Sure did and they told me you can forget it. If anything, they'll last longer than you. You heard about Rainbow at the Ebony Club last night?"

"Yeah, we heard. Now we're down to three."

"So, what do you want me to tell them?"

"I'll get back to you, RK, but I'm thinking it's not over until it's over."

On Friday night, Otis was walking toward his car in the warehouse district. He had been drinking half the night and enjoying the proceeds of knocking off those two hookers.

"Looks like there will be plenty more where that came from. This little war will be going on for some time," Spider said. Danyon wants more girls hit.

Only a few cars stood in the parking lot in the rear of the club because of the time of night. It was still hard to find his car in the corner of the lot, but he finally spotted it in a place where there was very little light. When he got near his car, two figures appeared from the back. Because he was drunk, he thought he was seeing double. After shaking his head, he realized it was in fact, two women. They were dressed all in black and carrying something in their hands. *Now, what the hell do these bitches want?* he thought. "Sorry ladies," he said. "I am in no shape for what you are selling. Catch me another time."

"Oh, that's all right," the taller one said. "We just want to give you a SWAK."

"A SWAK? What the hell is a SWAK?" At that moment, they unloaded both barrels on him with the two sawed off shotguns they carried. Because of his size, they loaded up and shot him twice more.

Eddie J Martin

Chapter 6

And then some

I WAS CALLED over to the five's apartment. Now, there were three. Danyon told me the situation and asked me if I had any suggestions. "Look they've already knocked out two out of the five of you, and they outnumber you 10 to 1. Plus, one of your hitmen is out. It should be clear to you to give it up. The next time I come here, I expect you'll be one less, or maybe even two."

Danyon looked at the others and said, "What do you guys think? If we give it up, we might as well move out of town right now and our reputation will follow us. Anybody want to be an auto mechanic?"

"No," Rabbit said, "but I don't want to end up like Rainbow either. We know what we were getting into when we had the girls hit, we underestimated them. We thought they were going to just roll over."

"So, what am I here for? I'm not in this shit."

54

"Yeah, you are in it, RK, whether you want to be or not," Danyon said. "You say that they have a hit squad? At least five of them?"

"That's right, and when you see the ladies in black coming, I'd go the other way."

"What about hitting them?" Trinidad asked.

"By the time you get to them, there won't be any of you left. Let's contact Spider and see if it's possible."

"I haven't heard from Spider since Otis got hit. I'm thinking he ran. First little sign of trouble, and he hits the road, even though things were going well and he was getting paid… Well, there are others we can get to take their jobs, that is, if you fellows want to continue this."

"I'm for staying," Rabbit said. "It's too late to find another job at this stage in my life."

"Maybe we need to handle this ourselves," Danyon said. "RK, what about you? Would you be interested in taking over Spider's job?"

"Absolutely not! I told you that from the start."

Three days later, Ingram walked into my office, looking better than ever. She sat down in one of my lounge chairs in front of my desk, crossed her legs, and just looked at me. "This is a pleasant surprise. What do I owe the pleasure of this visit?"

"Ms. Lynn wants to know whose side you are on."

"I'm on no one's side, Ingram. I have been a go-between from the start. Both groups agreed to it, so I don't understand the question."

"You had a meeting with the boys a few days ago, what did you talk about?"

"They talked about you and what they should do about you. I suggested that they give it up and go along with your suggestion, but they didn't see it that way."

"Is that all that went on in the meeting?"

"No, they offered me the job of helping get rid of you. I declined."

"That's all I wanted to know, Mr. Kane. One can't be too careful." She left and I wondered what her visit was about and whether they have been following me.

Two men got off the express train from Detroit, Michigan. They were dressed like Danyon, Trinidad and Rabbit. In fact, they were in the same business. They had heard about the predicament the guys in Cleveland were in and felt there was a void they could fill. They got right to work, hitting on the ladies who were out and noticed right away they weren't working for anyone. At two o'clock in the morning, they were approach by three ladies in black and were told they had to go back to Detroit. They were told they were in a 'no pimp' city. Of course, they had to be convinced at first but eventually, they understood something clearly at last.

CHAPER 7

At 2:30 AM in Ruben's girlfriend's bedroom, Ruben felt something pinch him on his leg. Once he woke up, he immediately thought it was Freda wanting a little early morning delight. He turned toward her, and as he did so, he saw two figures standing above him in black. One of them motioned for him to get dressed. He was relieved that Freda didn't wake up; she would have screamed her ass off.

In the car, Ingram sat in the backseat. "Hello, Mr. Kane. Sorry we woke you. I didn't think I'd be seeing you so soon but things are starting to heat up and so we need to step our game up."

And then some

"Would you like to tell me what you're talking about, Ingram?"

"Some people have been coming into the city, trying to fall into the void the previous people have created. But we won't let that happen, even if we must take out anyone who comes into town or wipe out the group that are here, or both."

"So, how can I help?"

"We will give them one last chance to get out of town."

"Get out of town? Has it come to that? What happened to the job offer?"

"I'm afraid that has passed. We want you to deliver this last message."

"Do I have a choice?"

"No, you don't, Mr. Kane. I promise this will be our last request. It will all be over soon."

Eddie J Martin

When I walked back up to the apartment, Freda was up and looking out the window.

"Ruben, who were those people?"

"Clients of mine. Go back to bed."

"They were here in the house; how did they get in?"

"They have their ways, Freda. Go back to bed."

"Danyon, this is Ruben. I've got a message from the ladies for you, and they say it will be their last."

"I've heard about as much as I want from those bitches. We already have people coming from out of town, trying to take over our shit. This is about to come to an end. Now, if they're willing to come to their senses, I'm willing to listen."

"So, you want me to tell them what?"

"Quote me, RK. Tell them to go fuck themselves. Fuck them all. We'll see them in hell first."

And then some

Rita called me from the outer office and told me there was a Miss Ingram on the line. I thanked her and said, "Yes, Ingram?"

"Did you deliver our message, Mr. Kane?"

"Yes, I did and you can imagine what the reply was."

"Well, thank you, Mr. Kane. You've done everything we've asked. We won't bother you again."

At the apartment, Danyon, Trinidad and Rabbit were putting a plan together on how to hit the ladies for the last time. They had found out where they were holding their meetings. Trinidad said he had contacted people from Chicago and they were just waiting for his call.

"They are willing to do whatever it takes to get it done. I contacted people from Louisiana and they're just waiting on our call," Rabbit chimed in. "Right now, the word is getting out that Cleveland is an open city. We can't have that."

"Has anybody heard what happened to Spider?" Trinidad said.

"Yeah, he was found on the train tracks west of here on the way to Chicago. His body was cut in half. They play dirty, don't they? Rabbit said."

"Well, we can expect no less, but then again, they learned from us," Danyon replied.

At that moment, the skylight burst in and three figures in black came through on ropes, holding machine guns and firing at Rabbit who was sitting at the bar. Another came through the back window and a fifth came up the elevator cable. Trinidad was sitting on the couch. He was hit ten times in the head, body and feet. Danyon was hit 22 times, mostly in the head and upper body from the ones coming in from the skylight. Rabbit, who was standing at the bar, took more than 18 rounds. After the bodies were checked, one of the ladies walked around with a Beretta and shot each one in the head. A nine-passenger van came up on the elevator and the ladies in black got in. The van went back down and another came up with six more girls in it, all dressed in coveralls. They started removing the bodies and cleaning up. Then, the vehicles were removed. After they were done and the apartment was back to its original state, the bodies were taken to Sue Lynn's funeral home and the cremation department.

A week later, the streets were back to normal, and the ladies were making more money than ever. Instead of pimps running around in their big flashy cars, there were five ladies riding around with SWAK bumper stickers and two-way radios in their cars. Men were still coming into the city trying to fill the void the boys had left behind but they were met at the station by SWAK and turned around. The ones that did try to put up a battle were met with swift justice and then some. Three months later, I received a call from Ingram. She asked me to stop by for a drink. I knew where she lived—she lived at Smooth's old place over by the river, where the boys used to reside. Oh, yeah. She called me Ruben.

Other books by this author:

Enlisted at 14…A Memoir

Enlisted at 14 and the Journey Continues

Enlisted at 14… Looking Back

Willow… A Novel

Eddie J Martin

Willow… One for the team

Willow… And the Medusa

Little Miss Willow… A Short Story

Assassin

Meet Ruben Kane

R.K. {Ruben Kane}

Ruben's Bag

Ruben's Bad Side

Smooth…A Ruben Kane novel

Mo Kane

Ducks in a Row

Just a Dream

Dream Catcher

And then some

Eddie J Martin